Katherine's Bike was Wonderfully Strange

BY JTK BELLE

Picklefish
Press

Copyright © 2018 by Picklefish Press

Printed in the United States of America
First Printing, 2017

ISBN 978-0-692-87279-6

JTK Belle is Jeff, Tommy, and Katie Belle.
Editor: Katie Belle
Creative Director: Tommy Belle
Book Design by Michelle M. White

Picklefish Press
www.picklefishpress.com

For
Lilly and Alethia

Katherine's bike was wonderfully strange.

When she shifted the gears the weather would change.

From first into second,
the wind would kick up.

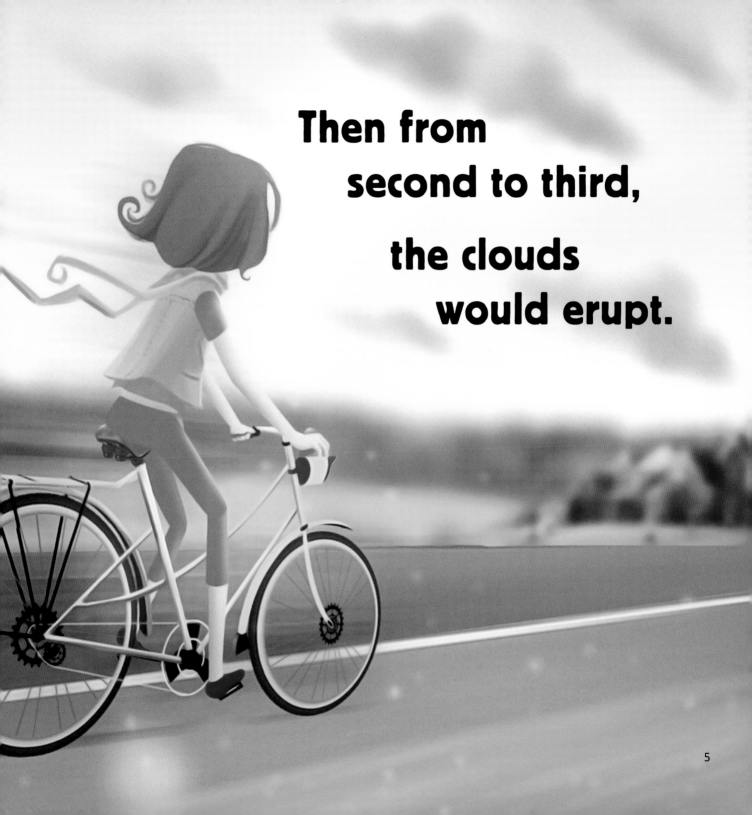

Then from
second to third,
the clouds
would erupt.

Around and
around and
around
went the chain.

**The faster
she pedaled,
the harder
it rained.**

**From third into fourth,
up spun a typhoon.**

And the faster she pedaled,
the harder it blew.

Over the bridge,
around and then under.

**The faster she pedaled,
the louder it thundered.**

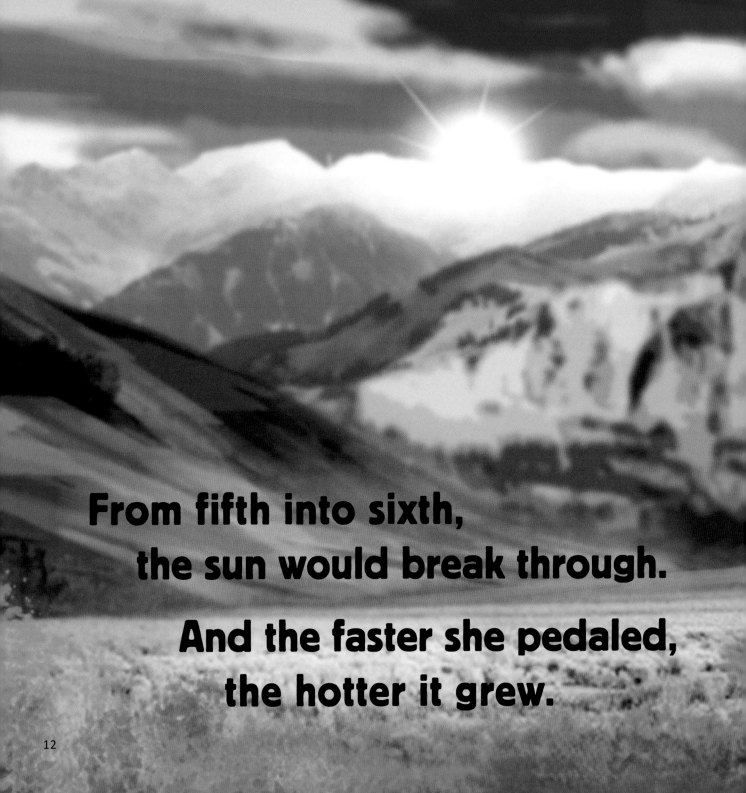

From fifth into sixth,
the sun would break through.

And the faster she pedaled,
the hotter it grew.

13

When she ran out of breath,
she had gone twenty miles.

So she tapped on the brakes
and she rested awhile.

15

She put down the kickstand
and lowered her feet.

And the sun disappeared
and so did the heat.

Then spinning the handles
around on their bars
while ringing the bells
would bring out the stars.

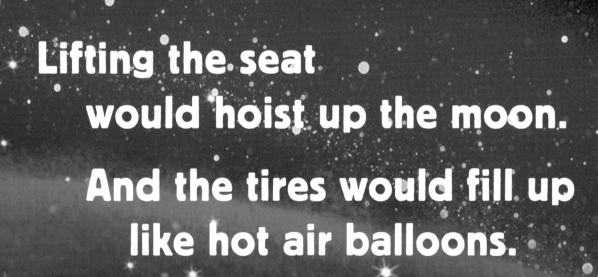

Lifting the seat
    would hoist up the moon.

And the tires would fill up
    like hot air balloons.

She floated up slowly
like smoke from a fire,
and balanced herself
like a bird on a wire.

She pedaled so high
    she could take in the view
of the neighborhood lights
    from the park to the zoo.

As she floated along
she lost track of the time,

'til she heard the sound
of the church bells chime.

And then she let out the air
from the big balloon tires

and floated down past
the telephone wires.

The stars were above and
her house was below her,
as the air from the tires
came out slower and slower.

She touched down in her yard
while they went on deflating...

**and ran into her house
where her dinner was waiting.**

JTK Belle
is Jeff, Tommy, and Katie Belle.
They live in Seattle, Washington.

 www.facebook.com/PicklefishPress

 www.twitter.com/jtkbelle

 www.picklefishpress.com

FREEDA THE CHEETAH

Kids love animals, and what child doesn't love a good game of hide-and-go-seek? But who is the world's very best player of hide-and-go-seek? Why, Freed the Cheetah, of course. Freeda the Cheetah of Mozambique.

As the elephant covers his eyes with his trunk and counts to a hundred, the animals of the savanna scatter in every direction. Elephant finds every one of them, from the hippo in the muddy water to the monkeys behind the bananas. But he just can't find that unfindable cheetah. Soon all the other animals join in on the search — even the lion and the blue wildebeests — as the colors of the savanna begin to fade into the evening. Will they find her before bedtime?

TOMMY O'TOM IN
A TUB O'TROUBLE

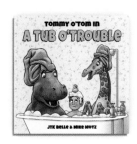

"Tommy O'Tom was taking a bath, when in walked a hippo and then a giraffe..."

In this charming bedtime read-aloud, written by JTK Belle in a laugh out-loud, rhythmic text, and beautifully-illustrated by Mike Motz, a bathtub full of mischievous zoo animals does their best to thwart Tommy O'Tom's bedtime preparations, and leave him to explain a bathroom mess to his puzzled mother. Recommended for ages 2-5.